Coleen
Style Queen

Sun, Sand & Sequins

HarperCollins *Children's Books*

With thanks to Lucy Courtenay

First published in Great Britain by HarperCollins *Children's Books* in 2008.
HarperCollins *Children's Books* is a division of HarperCollins *Publishers* Ltd,
77-85 Fulham Palace Road, Hammersmith, London, W6 8JB.

1

Text copyright © Coleen McLoughlin 2008
Illustrations by Nellie Ryan/EyeCandy and
Nicola Taylor NB Illustration 2008

ISBN-13 978-0-00-727742-1
ISBN-10 0-00-727742-3

Coleen
Style Queen

Sun, Sand & Sequins

One

OK, so holiday packing can be a struggle. Especially when you've got a mountain of clothes and shoes – not to mention an iPod, a camera and a hairdryer – to pack into a case roughly the size of a box of tissues. Oh, and did I mention that this particular suitcase is pink with gold sparkles?

"Mum!" I complained as Mum got my suitcase down from the loft and put it on my bed. "I can't take this on holiday. I'll get laughed off the beach!"

"You loved it when you were seven, and I'm

sure you can love it again, Coleen," said Mum.

I sighed and flipped the case open. Then I packed my favourite summer shoes: a pair of sparkly sandals covered in silver sequins. They fitted – with about three millimetres left over. "But I'll never get everything in!" I wailed, looking at the other six pairs that I'd lined up on my bedroom floor.

"What do you need seven pairs of shoes for?" Dad asked, stopping at my room and staring at my packing. There was something bright orange draped over his arm. "We're going for a *beach* holiday, Coleen – tomorrow, ideally, though at the rate you're going you won't be packed until Tuesday. Are you planning to paddle in a different pair of shoes every day?"

I rolled my eyes at him. Dads don't *get* shoes. "What's that?" I asked, eyeing the orange thing on Dad's arm.

"Ta-da!" Dad announced, unfurling the most

disgusting pair of orange swimming trunks I'd ever seen and flapping them at me. "What do you think?"

"The fish in the sea'll think you're a giant Wotsit, Dad," I advised. "Think again."

"At least you lot won't lose me at the hotel pool," Dad joked, folding up his shorts again.

"Believe me, Dad, we will," I muttered as Dad went off to help Mum squeeze everything into their old black case on wheels. "As quickly as we can."

My little sister, Em, wandered into my room and flopped down on the bed. As usual, she looked a total mess. Football strip (badly in need of a wash), football socks and a pair of trackie bottoms with holes in the knees, not to mention a gap in her front teeth where a tooth had just dropped out.

"And there was me, thinking seven-year-old girls wore pink all day long," I sighed.

"Yuck," said Em, as I knew she would. Needless to

say, her suitcase had the emblem of her favourite footie team, Marshalswick Park, on it.

"Get out of here, Em," I begged, trying to decide between three different T-shirts. "Haven't you got packing to do?"

"All done," Em smirked.

"What?" I shrieked, dropping my tees. "But you only started about five minutes ago!"

Em shrugged. "Cozzie, T-shirts, shorts, sandals, latest football mag, autograph book because footballers go to the Algarve and you never know, toothbrush," she recited. "Didn't take long."

"What about knickers?" I demanded.

Em wrinkled her forehead. "Oh yeah," she said, getting off my bed, "I'd better stick in a couple of pairs."

8

Holidays in my family usually go like this. Mum goes on at Dad for weeks to book something. The holidays get closer. Dad doesn't do anything until the last minute, and then he grabs the cheapest thing he sees, which nearly always has flights leaving at four o'clock in the morning. Mum's left running around like a mad thing, getting Nan to take Rascal our dog and vacuuming behind the couch. Well, this time, Dad has totally outdone himself. He booked us a week in the Algarve this afternoon – and we are getting a taxi to the airport before sunrise tomorrow morning.

"Heaven knows what this place is going to be like," Mum grumbled as we all grabbed a bite to eat before what was going to be the shortest night's sleep in history.

"It's the Algarve, Trish," Dad said soothingly. "Sea, sand and plenty of sun. I tell you, I can spot the good ones a mile off. When have I ever been wrong?"

"Well," Mum started, "how about that time we went to Croatia and the hotel hadn't even been built? Or the trip to Brittany that turned out to be a trip to Britain, which I didn't want to visit because *I already lived there*? Or—"

"Well, this one's going to be different," Dad interrupted hastily. "Trust me."

Em and I shared a look. We'd believe *that* once we got there.

It felt like I'd only just shut my eyes when Mum was shaking me awake again. I whittled my shoes down to three pairs and jumped on my sparkly pink case to shut it. I squeezed another T-shirt, scarf and belt into my hand luggage and put on as many extra clothes as I could. Then I think I actually fell asleep in the taxi, because suddenly it was all lights and

bustle and that ding-dong echo you get in airports. Now my eyelids were officially open, it was time to get excited.

Airports are brilliant places. They just *smell* of holidays. There's so many different kinds of people to look at, making me wonder about all the different places they must be travelling to. Tall ones, skinny ones, rich ones, ones with tans that make them look like old leather handbags and ones so pale you just know they'll burn to a crisp on their holiday beach within seconds. And if you ever need fashion inspiration, the mix of colours and styles in an airport is full of it!

As we waited around for our flight to be called, I browsed through the gorgeous duty-free clothes shops and dashed off a couple of postcards to my best mates, Mel and Lucy. I'd barely had a chance to tell them I was off for a whole week. It would be really weird not having them there to gossip with. Then I thought of Ben, Lucy's big brother, as I posted the cards. I'd had a crush on him for half my life. He'd just had a dramatic and final break-up with his on-off girlfriend Jasmine, and I was hoping that a week in the Portuguese sun would give me the sort of tan that would make him notice me at long last...

"Flight TP051 for Faro," droned the tannoy after we'd been there about two hours. "Departing from gate twelve. Would passengers please make their way to..."

"So far so good, eh?" Dad said as we all filed on board and took our seats near the front of the plane.

Mum muttered something about chickens and eggs. Em clambered across to the window seat and pulled out her new football magazine.

"If you're going to read that," I pointed out, "how come you get the window seat?"

"No arguments, kids," Dad said. "You can have the

window on the way home, Coleen. This is our holiday now, and I plan to enjoy it."

Kids! I scowled at Dad. Ignoring me, he took out his fitness magazine, and I could see him sucking in his stomach as he looked at the muscly bloke on the front cover.

"What do you think of my stomach, Trish?" he asked Mum, sounding a bit anxious.

"Squishy," said Mum. Her nose was already deep in a pink, sparkly novel that was guaranteed to be all about kissing tall dark strangers. "But nice."

"Just as well you like it, Mum," I said, settling back into my seat as the plane started taxiing down the runway. I jabbed the cover of Dad's mag. "Coz there's no way it's ever gonna look like *that*."

We flew through a clear blue sky, with Em giving us Fascinating Factoids about Portugal and football practically the whole way. Apparently the whole country is mad for it. No wonder my little sister was excited that we were going there.

"*And* half the Marshalswick Park squad have holiday homes in the Algarve," Em said happily, folding up her magazine as the plane started its descent into Faro airport. "That must mean it's brilliant."

As I've said before, Marshalswick Park are Em's favourite team. They'd risen up the league like a rocket ever since they'd taken on this new manager, and now they were serious contenders for the top spot – as Em told us most weekends after watching their matches on the telly.

We got through baggage control and came out into the bright Portuguese sun. I whipped out my new sunnies and stuck them on my nose as our rep ushered us all on to a big, air-conditioned bus that stood outside the airport underneath these waving palm trees.

"See?" said Dad smugly as we all settled back into our comfy seats and watched the driver and his mates packing our luggage into the big locker underneath the bus. "I told you everything would be OK."

The bus wound out of the airport. After about fifteen minutes, it pulled off the dual carriageway into the first resort: a buzzy-looking place with loads of bars and extremely tall hotels.

"Not us," said Dad as the bus doors slammed shut and we drove on.

"Shame," Mum sighed. "It looked like fun."

We stopped off at three more places along the way. The bus was getting emptier and emptier, and still the rep hadn't read out our names.

"Are we going to Spain?" Em complained after the fourth place came and went.

The bus put on its ticker and pulled off the main road again.

"Castelo do Sol," I said, reading out the town's name as we swung past a sign and a bunch of half-built hotels that had Mum looking tense. "What do you think that means?"

"Sol Campbell's castle!" Em gasped.

Doesn't that girl ever think of *anything* but football?!

The bus squeezed down an impossibly narrow lane that had me flinching back from the windows, thinking the mirrors were going to scrape the buildings on both sides. Then it pulled out again on to this long beachfront road. There were three massive hotels all stood next to each other, with pools and sea views across a gorgeous sandy beach. The road was fringed with palm trees, and these brilliant rock formations stood down by the shore like huge golden statues.

"It's magic!" I breathed, staring at the beach in delight.

"I take back everything bad I've ever said about you, Kieran," said Mum, staring up at the hotels. Their polished marble walls shone in the sun like glass, and their pools winked through the bus windows at us like pale blue sapphires.

The bus dropped three lots of totally ecstatic-looking holidaymakers outside the three hotels. There was only one family left as we swung away from the seafront.

Us.

"Hotel Paraíso," said the rep, snapping her little notebook shut as the bus gave a very final-sounding wheeze and stopped at the side of the road. "That'll be you lot, then. Save the best for last, eh?"

We stared at the place the bus had brought us. The water-stained red and white awning over the main entrance flapped at us in an embarrassed kind of way, and the words *Hotel Paraíso* flickered in blue

17

neon letters across the front of the once-maybe-white-but-now-grey building.

"*Paraíso* means 'paradise'," offered the rep.

There was a beat of silence.

"Kie*RAN*!" Mum yelled.

Two

"What do you want me to do, Trish?" Dad protested as the bus whooshed off down the road, leaving us outside the Hotel Paraíso with our luggage around our feet. "You heard what she said. There's nowhere else!"

"You're *never* booking us another holiday, Kieran," Mum shouted. "I'll give all the travel agents in Hartley your photo and order them not to serve you. And if I see you anywhere near the Internet, I'll cut up your bankcard."

"I like it," said Em, staring up at the hotel. "It looks friendly."

"Friendly if you're a rat or a flea, maybe," Mum yelled. "*Honestly*, Kieran…"

I looked at the hotel while Mum ranted on. I could see what Em meant. OK, so it wasn't made of glass and marble, and there was no sea view. But the windows shone like someone had taken the trouble to clean them, even though the building itself looked like it hadn't had a new coat of paint in years. The flickering blue letters spelling out the hotel's name were naff – not to mention broken – but it was on the sunny side of the street, and it seemed quiet.

"…and I can't believe a place like this even has a *pool*…"

"Mum doesn't half go on," Em said. She picked up her Marshalswick Park suitcase and pushed open the hotel door.

Mum stopped shouting. Even when she gets mad, she doesn't like upsetting strangers – like the hotel manager we were about to meet. She and Dad stiffly followed me and Em inside.

Some soft guitar music was playing in the small, blue-tiled reception area. There was a dark-haired man with a thick black moustache standing at the reception desk, along with two other people: a kind-looking dark-haired woman and a lad about my age. I did a double-take at him. He had gorgeous soft-tanned skin, black hair that curled around his shoulders and these huge brown eyes with eyelashes like you see on really pretty cows. I had this awful feeling that I was staring, but I couldn't help myself. He was the cutest thing I'd ever seen.

"Welcome to Castelo do Sol," said the manager, stepping forward and shaking Mum and Dad's hands with both of his own. If he'd heard them rowing out on the pavement, he didn't show it. "We hope that you will have a very nice stay with us. I am Antonio Santos. Please allow me to present my wife Ana, and my son João."

The way Mr Santos said *João* made it sound like *sh-wow. Wow's dead on*, I thought as I stared at the lad, who was now shaking hands with Mum and Dad.

"Hi," João said as he reached me. He was taller than me, which wasn't exactly surprising as I'm quite little, and his smile was white and gorgeous against his brown skin.

"Hi," I squeaked back. I was so knocked out by how beautiful he was that I almost forgot to take the hand he was holding out to me. Then, when I remembered, I shook it so hard I practically took his arm off at the elbow. This awful blush started sweeping up my cheeks – I could feel it. Em noticed and giggled.

Mum was beginning to thaw out at our polite welcome. Mr Santos led us up the narrow tiled staircase to our rooms. I followed on. Then something made me turn my head back for another look at João. He was carrying our luggage a few steps behind us. As he grinned at me I fell up the next two slightly wonky steps and grazed my knee.

"Here, I will help you," said João, pulling me to my feet.

"Are you OK, Coleen?" Em smirked.

"Fine," I muttered, blushing even harder than before.

"...very quiet rooms at the back," Mr Santos was saying to Mum, opening the bedroom door. "Please let us know if there are any problems. This is for your girls." And he gave this lovely little bow, letting me and Em in and taking Mum and Dad to the next door along.

The room was whitewashed, with pale yellow blankets on the beds and slatted wooden shutters on the window. João put our suitcases on the waxed wooden floor. "Nice bag," he grinned as he set the pink sparkly monster down. He spoke great English, with this adorable accent. "It's yours?" he asked, raising his eyebrows at Em.

"As *if*!" Em said, looking offended. "It's my sister Coleen's."

"Cheers, Em," I muttered, snatching up my sparkly case as João left the room. "Now he thinks I'm a weird pink-suitcase freak as well as a clumsy, blushing idiot."

"Chill *out*, Coleen," Em said, rolling her eyes at me. She flipped her suitcase over, tipped out its pathetic contents and shoved everything into a drawer. "Unpacked," she announced, slinging her case under her bed and flopping down with her football magazine.

I stared at the contents of the pink suitcase. For a minute I couldn't work out what I was looking at.

"This isn't mine," I said at last, pulling out a floaty white dress and holding it up in confusion. "What…"

I upended the case over my bed. A whole bunch of stuff fell out that I'd never seen before. "I don't believe it!" I wailed, rifling through everything. "Where are my sequinned sandals? Where's my new swimsuit?" It was the cutest swimsuit you ever saw, blue with red and white spots and this little white frill around the legs that was totally nautical and now.

"Hey," said Em, glancing up from her magazine. "What are the chances of two pink-suitcase freaks sharing the same plane today?"

"Mum!" I went running down the corridor to share my suitcase disaster. "I've got the wrong…"

Mum and Dad were standing in their room arguing. Mum was holding a threadbare towel that looked as if it had seen better days.

"…ever so polite and I know it's clean and

everything," Mum was saying, "but you don't expect holes in towels, do you? You need to get on to our rep and *insist* on changing hotels, Kieran."

"You can't change hotels now," I said, stopping in their doorway as a wave of dismay flooded through me. "They're ever so nice, Mum. What will they think?"

"I'm sorry, Coleen," Mum said. "I know Mr Santos and his family have been very welcoming, but this is our holiday and I expect certain standards." She held up the towel between her fingers. "I don't mean to be unkind, but I wouldn't dry our dishes with this."

Dad looked harassed. "I think we should give it a go tonight, Trish," he said. "We're all tired and I need a shower. Let's give it a chance, and if you're still not happy in the morning, I'll talk to the rep about moving. OK?"

Mum sat down on the bed with a sigh as Dad

26

disappeared into the tiny little en-suite bathroom and shut the door.

"Mum," I said, remembering about my suitcase fiasco. "I've got the wrong bag. There's all this gear I've never seen before. What am I going to do?"

Mum sighed and shook her head. "Whatever next? I don't know, Coleen," she said. "Is there a name on the suitcase?"

I shook my head. "I didn't put my name on mine either," I confessed.

Mum did this hard-breathing thing through her nose, which is always a sign that she's about to lose it. "Your dad can report it to the rep and she can try and track down your bag," she said. "But in the meantime, you'll just have to wear what you're wearing right now."

"Every *day*?" I said, aghast. I loved what I had on: hot pink cropped trousers, a little skirt over the top, a grey hoodie with pink piping around the edge, a white T-shirt over a yellow vest and white Converse trainers. And I did have that extra T-shirt and a few accessories in my hand luggage. But as anyone knows, even the best clothes get seriously dull after a couple of days. "Mum—"

"It's either that or wear this other person's clothes," Mum snapped. "Now, I've got a headache, Coleen. Go and see what Em's up to. When your dad's finished in the shower, we'll go and find something to eat, OK?"

I trailed back to our room, telling myself that the rep would find my bag before the end of the week. Trying really hard not to cry as I wondered if I'd ever see my favourite sandals again, I stared at the mystery person's luggage on my bed. Then I started sorting it out. White dress, white shorts, green T-shirt with a hideous logo on the front. Grey leggings.

Grey leggings, on a summer holiday? I packed it all away again and slammed the suitcase shut. There was no *way* I was wearing that lot.

Great. Stuck in one style for my entire holiday. What would João think when he saw me looking exactly the same every single day?

Me and Em both leaped out of our skins as we heard Dad yell: "OWWW!"

"What happened?" Em demanded, dashing down the corridor and charging into Mum and Dad's room with me hot on her heels. "Did you find a dead mouse?"

Dad was standing in the middle of the room, dripping wet and wrapped in a towel that looked even more threadbare than the one Mum had been waving around. In his hand was something that looked suspiciously like a shower tap. There was shampoo still in his hair, sticking up in white bubbly clumps.

"It came off in my hand," he said. "The shower went

scalding hot and there was nothing I could do about it!"

Mum snatched the tap off Dad. "That's the final straw, Kieran," she said. "We have to take this up with Mr Santos and then move hotels. Before tonight, if possible. Em? Coleen? I hope you haven't unpacked yet?"

"I haven't got anything to unpack, have I?" I pointed out grumpily. I couldn't believe how badly this holiday was turning out. Not only had I lost my suitcase, but we would leave the Hotel Paraíso forever and I'd never see João again. And even if we *did* see him, he wouldn't speak to us because we'd walked out of his hotel. And I was stuck in one pair of trousers all week. Life just wasn't fair.

Mum looked like a bull on the rampage. As Dad struggled to rub the rest of the shampoo out of his hair with the threadbare towel, me and Em followed Mum down the stairs.

"Mr Santos," said Mum, banging the shower tap

down on the reception desk. "We've got a *serious* problem with our shower."

Mr Santos's smile wavered at the edges. "I'm so very sorry, *Senhora*," he said, looking flustered as he took the tap off Mum. He turned and rattled something off in very fast Portuguese at his wife, who dashed for the telephone.

Mum was shaking her head. "I'm very sorry too," she said, "but we can't stay here, Mr Santos. Broken taps, dreadful towels. This isn't what we were expecting. I think it's best if we leave."

Mr Santos's moustache quivered. He looked like he was about to cry. "Please, *Senhora*," he said, "my cousin, he is a plumber. My wife is calling him now. We will fix your shower *imediatamente*. There will be new towels in your room tonight. And please, with our apologies, you must come for dinner at our restaurant tonight, free of charge."

"Well…" Mum wavered. She's always a sucker where food is concerned.

"My wife, she makes the best *bacalhau* in Castelo do Sol," Mr Santos said, taking Mum's hand. "You will taste it tonight."

João appeared at Mr Santos's side, looking nearly as worried as his dad. I so wanted to see his gorgeous white smile again.

"Let's stay, Mum," I begged. "Mr Santos is doing his best to help us."

"I don't know, Coleen…" Mum began.

"What's *bacalhau*?" Em asked.

"Codfish," said Mr Santos.

"Like cod and chips?" Em said, brightening. Cod and chips was her favourite.

"More like your fish pie, maybe," Mr Santos explained.

Em beamed. Fish pie was her next favourite.

 32

"You will fix the shower for us this afternoon?" Mum checked.

"*Claro que sim*," Mr Santos nodded, shaking her hand vigorously. "For sure. And the towels too. Tonight, eight o'clock, you will eat for free in our restaurant. You will not regret it, *Senhora*."

"Right," said Mum, making a decision with the deepest sigh you ever heard. "We'll stay tonight. But if things don't improve, Mr Santos, we are leaving in the morning."

I almost cheered and hugged her on the spot. We were staying! Well – for now at least...

Three

O nce Dad had got the soap out of his hair in mine and Em's shower, we all got ready for the beach.

"What am I going to wear for swimming?" I asked Mum as we left our keys with a very relieved Mr Santos and headed down the dusty street towards the sea. I'd taken off my hoodie, my overskirt and my white T-shirt, and with my yellow vest and pink cropped trousers I *almost* felt like I was in a new outfit.

"We'll buy you something to swim in, love," Mum said, sounding mellow as the lovely sun warmed

her shoulders. "This place looks like it might have some nice shops."

It did. Out on the seafront, rows of little boutiques faced the beach with the most adorable – and expensive – beach outfits you ever saw. For visitors with a little less cash, there were kaftans and bikinis, sunhats and flip-flops all lined along the front, where colourful gypsy ladies had set up market stalls while their husbands tipped black hats over their eyes and snoozed away in the sun. I picked out a brown and white striped swimsuit and a brown straw hat, which I clamped straight on to my head.

Maybe losing my luggage wasn't such a bad thing after all, I mused happily as we headed down on to the sand. Kicking off my trainers, I tied the laces together and slung them around my neck, loving the feeling of the boiling hot sand between my toes.

We found a kiosk that sold hot little beefsteaks in a

bun, kind of like a hamburger but chewier. With lots of ketchup and mustard, they filled us up perfectly, leaving just enough room for an ice cream. Em and I laughed ourselves sick at the sight of a holey yellow ice cream called a "Cheesy" on the side of the kiosk. Sadly they didn't have any in the freezer!

Mum and Dad found a great little spot by one of the big rock formations, where there was just enough shade for all of us when the sun got too strong. And after slathering ourselves with suncream, we all tried a bit of paddling. The water was colder than I was expecting, but after the heat of the sand it was completely gorgeous.

"Psst!" Em nudged me as I snoozed happily underneath my new brown hat. "Look who's over there!"

I pushed my hat up with one thumb and stared across at where a game of beach football was taking

place on a specially laid-out pitch, with seats running around the sides. Nipping in and out of a bunch of shouting, laughing lads was João Santos.

Em jumped up.

"Where are you going?" I said in alarm, although I already knew the answer.

"To play football with João, of course," Em said over her shoulder. "Mum? Dad? Can I go?"

Our folks gave a couple of sleepy grunts that sounded like yes.

"Watch out for Em, will you Coleen love?" Mum mumbled, opening one eye to check where the game was taking place before closing it again.

"You can't interrupt their game, Em," I warned as I got to my feet.

"Of course I can," Em said. "Anyway, their right wing is rubbish. I can do better than that."

When Em gets an idea in her head, she's like a

little bulldozer, knocking down everything in her path to get where she wants to go. And while she's a brilliant right wing for Hartley Juniors, our local under-eights football team, the game she was marching towards was made up of lads five years older than her and, in some cases, twice as tall.

"Em!" I hissed, struggling through the hot, slippery sand after her. "Don't barge in! You'll make me look stupid!"

"You won't look stupid," Em said. "How many of these lads have ever seen a girl play like I can? And you're my sister, so you'll be dead popular."

It's safe to say that among all the seven-year-old girls that I've ever met, Em's unique. Even when she says stuff like that, it doesn't come out as boasting. It just comes out like it's true. Which it usually is. Resigned to the fact that this was about to get embarrassing, I stopped at the edge of the game and watched as Em jumped over the pitch-side seats and headed towards João like a little whirlwind of tangled brown hair and ancient purple swimming cozzie.

"Hi," she announced, just as João was about to kick the ball to one of his mates.

The other lads started laughing and whistling as João mis-kicked. To João's credit, he didn't turn all nasty on Em for making him look silly. Instead he picked up the ball and smiled at her. "Hi. Emma, yes?" he said.

"Call me Em," she said, taking the ball out of João's hand and lining it up efficiently on the sand. "And you got the side-spin all wrong on that kick. You should've done it like this."

She demonstrated. The ball soared off the sand and landed smack in the opposite goal, leaving the tall, spotty goalie looking totally dumbfounded.

All the lads suddenly clustered around Em

like she was some sort of miracle that had appeared out of nowhere.

"Where do you learn to kick that way?"

"Girls, they play football in England?"

João glanced around at me as Em got chatting to the rest of the lads. I walked as casually as I could on to the pitch.

"Hiya," I said. *Stay cool,* I told myself firmly as I felt myself wobble. "Sorry about my sister. She's football crazy."

"She's crazy good," João said admiringly. "She has maybe just eight years?"

My stomach was in danger of bouncing right out of my mouth.

"She's seven," I said. "And totally mad."

João laughed. "I can see," he said. "You play football?"

I shook my head. "Fashion and music's more my line," I confessed.

"You like surfing?" João asked.

I was surprised at the question. "I don't know," I said. "I've never tried it." I glanced out at the sea, where a line of surfers bobbed among the waves. It looked pretty fun.

The game was starting again, this time with Em right in the middle of it all.

"I'm glad that you are staying," said João to me. He gave me this cute little half-smile, his dark brown eyes meeting mine for what felt like ages. Then he jogged back to rejoin the game.

I sat down on one of the seats beside the little pitch and hugged my knees close to my chest. Something inside me felt like it was about to explode, but in the nicest way you can imagine. I think João liked me!

I watched the rest of the game in daydreaming heaven.

"João's totally brilliant," Em announced, flopping down on the seat beside me after nearly an hour of running about. "I wish he could come and live in England and play football with me all day long."

João and the rest of the lads came and sat with us. A couple of them gave Em high fives.

"This is Zeca, this is Carlos, this is Paulo and this is Nuno." Em introduced everyone, waving her hand around the footballing gang. "Guys, this is my sister Coleen."

Now I knew what Em meant about her making me popular. The lads were all puffed out from their footie and dead interested in us and England.

"I want live in England," said Nuno, who looked a couple of years younger than the rest of the lads.

"I think the weather in Hartley would disappoint you," I joked. "And we don't have a beach like this on our doorstep."

"Is not so good here either," said Zeca, the tall spotty lad who'd been in goal. "No money."

The others murmured agreement.

"What?" I said in surprise. I glanced back at the huge, gleaming hotels on the seafront. "What about those hotels? And all those shops?"

João looked serious. "We don't like these hotels so much," he said. "They make persons like my father lose his business. All the tourists and their money go to the big hotels and not to us. Things were different before they came to Castelo do Sol. It is harder now."

I felt a wave of shame as I remembered how excited we had been when we saw the big hotels on the waterfront, and how disappointed we'd felt on seeing Hotel Paraíso. "Broken taps and old towels," I said as I understood.

João made a face. "Broken taps, *exacto*," he nodded.

Dad appeared at the side of the pitch. "Game over, is it?" he asked, looking disappointed.

"Too late, Dad," said Em. "Bad luck. Tomorrow, guys, yeah?" she said to the footballers. "And can my dad play next time?"

It was amazing the way my little sister had all these big lads in the palm of her hand. Nodding and agreeing enthusiastically, they all clapped Em on the shoulder and ruffled her hair. Then they nodded at me and shook Dad's hand before heading away from the pitch and back to their homes.

"Nice lads," Dad commented as we all walked back to where Mum was still sunbathing by the big rock. The tide was coming in now, and it wouldn't be long before Mum's towel got a soaking. "Nice place, too. I'm so relaxed, I can hardly believe it was only this morning we were at home."

"Brilliant place," Em agreed, clinging on to Dad's

hand. "Can we always come here on holiday, Dad?"

I glanced over to where I could still just see João jogging up the beach and back towards the Hotel Paraíso. It was time to rev up my brain and figure out a way of making some extra money for the Hotel Paraíso so that Mr Santos could get new taps instead of always having to fix up the old ones. And I admit it – I also wanted João to smile at me again, just the way he'd smiled on the pitch and made my chest go all tight and brilliant.

Four

The sun was starting to dip down behind the edge of the cliffs when we finally dragged ourselves away from the beach. The tide had come in almost as far as the beach-football pitch, and was now on the way out again. It left behind these stretches of perfectly smooth sand which made me want to run out and leave my footprints all over it. The tide thing was different from Spain, where we'd been before.

Back at the hotel, Mr Santos looked delighted to see us again. *"Senhor! Senhora!"* he cried. "And the

46

senhoritas too! You have a good time on our beautiful beach? João tells me that your young girl plays football like a champion."

Dad beamed. He coaches Em's team back in Hartley, so anyone with a good word about Em's footie skills is a mate for life. "She's our champion all right," he said, unable to resist a little boast. "Top goal scorer for Hartley Juniors this season."

Mr Santos whistled. The two men launched into a football chat right there and then, with Em joining in for all she was worth. To my delight, João popped out from the back room and joined in the chat as well, his hair all slicked back from a shower. He darted these little looks at me every now and then.

"Football," said Mum, shaking her head as we listened to them going on about leagues and penalties and the European Champions League.

"It's a whole language of its own. Come on, love," she said to me. "Let's go and get changed."

The tap was back on in Mum and Dad's bathroom, and newer-looking towels had been laid out on everyone's beds. Mum and I took turns in the shower, chatting about girl stuff.

"João seems like a nice lad," said Mum, rubbing her hair dry as I hopped in the shower after her.

I turned the tap on and tilted my blushing face up to the hot jet of water. "He's all right," I mumbled.

"He seems to like you," Mum said.

"You think?" I poked my head out around the shower curtain, unable to resist asking.

Mum just smiled at me. "So," she said, changing the subject, "what are you going to wear then?"

"Well, there's the pink trousers, the pink trousers or the pink trousers," I said, feeling both relieved and disappointed that we weren't talking about João any more as I wrapped myself up in my new towel.

"Come on, my little fashion queen!" Mum said, putting on a nice pair of white jeans and a pale blue top that matched her eyes. "Aren't you always saying you could improvise a whole new wardrobe out of a curtain and pair of socks?"

"Hardly!" I giggled, picturing the end result: gross!

"You know what I mean," Mum laughed. "This is a chance to be inventive, Coleen. Make the best of it."

I thought about what Mum had said as I walked back to our room. Maybe I *could* improvise a whole different look every day, just with what I'd got. I laid out everything I had on the bed and took a long, hard look. Maybe – just maybe – there *were* a few wardrobe surprises I could pull off before our rep found my suitcase and brought it back to me.

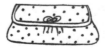

"I've never seen that top before," Dad commented as we all gathered back in the reception area, ready for our food.

"You have, Dad," I grinned. "Just not like this."

I'd made myself a great little top out of the scarf I'd stuck in my hand luggage at the last minute: looping it around my neck, then criss-crossing over at the front and tying it around my waist at the back. With the skirt I'd worn over my trousers on the flight that morning, it worked really well. And my trainers looked kind of funky, even though I'd never have thought of putting trainers on with this skirt before.

The restaurant was really sweet, with a bar, about eight little tables all laid with white cloths and glass vases full of bright pink papery flowers that Mum said was called bougainvillea. Like the rest of the hotel, there were loads of blue and white tiles on the walls, and the wooden floor shone with a nice-smelling wax. A glass door opened out to a sunny courtyard at the back, with the same papery flowers as in the restaurant vases growing up the walls all around us like a crazy pink explosion.

"The best seat in the house," said Mr Santos, showing us to a table beside a little trickling water feature.

João was our waiter tonight. As he took our order for drinks, I guessed that the hotels on the front weren't run by families in the same way as this one. It reminded me of the promise I'd made to myself: to think of how to make some extra money for the Hotel Paraíso this summer.

"Everyone is happy to have the *bacalhau*?" Mr Santos checked with us.

"If you say it's good, we'll give it a go," said Dad.

We sat for a bit, watching the birds swooping around in the courtyard. They kept dipping down to

the little water feature beside our table to drink and splash their feathers.

"I must say, for all the problems, I like it here," said Mum, leaning back on her chair with the glass of cold white wine that João had brought her. "It may not be all ritz and glitz, but maybe it's the better for all that. I do wish it had a pool though."

"We've got the sea," I put in. "We don't need a pool, Mum."

I was so keen to keep Mum thinking about the Hotel Paraíso's good points that I slurped my Coke a bit too fast so I could join in the conversation. Predictably, this massive burp came out.

"João heard that," Em said as Mum and Dad tutted at my manners.

I spun around on my chair, appalled. "He never!"

But João was nowhere to be seen.

"Sucker," Em chirped, and ducked as I tried to hit her.

"The proof of the pudding is in the eating, as they say," said Dad, looking up as João came towards us with a tray. "Or the bacal-wotsit, come to that."

"*Bacalhau a casa do Santos*," said João, putting down four little pottery bowls. "Codfish, Santos-style."

I dug in. It was salty, but the creaminess balanced it out and made it totally delicious. There were herbs and little pickles too that matched the fish brilliantly.

"Mmm," said Dad after a minute, his mouth full of food.

"Mmm-*mmm*," added Mum, her mouth even fuller.

"Mum, can you do fish pie like this next time?" Em mumbled.

"That was *cracking*," said Dad across to Mrs Santos as he finished up his bowl.

Hovering at the glass door back into the restaurant, Mrs Santos looked worried.

"He means good," I grinned, and Mrs Santos's face changed from worry to pleasure.

As the evening darkened, little candles were lit on the tables. A few more people came in, and Mr Santos greeted them all by name. I realised that they were locals.

"Why aren't there any other tourists?" Mum wondered, obviously realising the same thing as me. "Or any other guests apart from us?"

Dad was scraping away at the side of his little bowl of cinnamon rice pudding that had come for dessert. "Beats me," he said, licking the spoon. "Best holiday grub I've ever had."

"Advertising," said Em wisely. "They've not got anything about this place out on the pavement. How are the tourists supposed to know about it?"

Even though it was getting late and we'd all been awake for hours, I didn't feel tired. It was magic out

 54

in that courtyard, with the flickering candles and the trickling water and the strange foreign chatter we could hear all around us. I pushed Em's comment about advertising around my head. We needed some kind of event for the Hotel Paraíso – something where Mr Santos could advertise his business and his restaurant so that all the tourists in Castelo do Sol got to know about Mrs Santos's brilliant cooking.

As I was thinking this through some lovely music spilled across the courtyard. One of the locals had just finished his food and had now taken out this amazing guitar with a long neck and a round, fat body. It made a beautiful sound that made me think of waterfalls.

Mrs Santos came out of the restaurant with a tea-towel slung over her shoulder. To our amazement, she nodded at the guitar player, opened her mouth and started singing. Right there on the spot! Tea-towel and everything! It was crazy, but brilliant at the same time – like nothing mattered except the music.

"Everything OK?" João was standing at our table, ready to collect our empty plates.

"Perfect," said Mum warmly. "Tell your mother that I must get that recipe from her."

João laughed. "My mother's *bacalhau* is the biggest secret in Castelo do Sol!" he said. "She will never tell you how she makes it."

As he piled our plates on to his tray, he glanced shyly at me. "Coleen?" he said. "Do you want to come to the beach tomorrow in the morning with me?"

I almost dropped the plate I was handing to him. "Yes, yeah, I would, yes!" I said.

"I think maybe just *three* 'yes'es would've got the message across," Em said as João beamed and went back into the restaurant. "You didn't need four, Col."

I sat at our table in a daze. João had just asked me

to the beach. Our first date! We'd paddle along the shore! We'd hold hands! We'd...

"Lovely," said Dad. "You can take Em with you, Col. Give your mum and me a bit of a lie-in."

Five

So there I was, out on my first *ever* date – with my little sister tagging along. Great.

It was a gorgeous morning. There was a little breeze washing along the street outside the hotel, rustling through the bougainvillea that seemed to grow everywhere in the town. I decided to make the best of things and had put on my new brown and white swimsuit and hat, with yesterday's scarf tied around my middle like a sarong. Dad had spoken to our rep last night, but she still hadn't found my case. Typical.

"It's a good day for waves," João said as he came into the reception area with two little surfboards tucked under his arm. He was wearing a wetsuit which made him look like a little brown-skinned seal. "You want to try some body-boarding?"

"What's body-boarding?" Em wanted to know as we headed out of the hotel and down towards the beach.

"It's like surfing, but you lie on the board," João explained, showing us his two boards. "The board is smaller than a surfboard, see?"

There were quite a lot of people down by the water already. The breeze had whipped up the waves, which broke in frilly white lines along the sand.

"I don't have a wetsuit," I said, staring at the sea and wondering how cold it was.

"No problem," João said. "My cousin Pedro has two extra suits. I asked him to meet us here today."

Pedro looked about fourteen. His skin was darker

than João's, and his hair was cut really short. The suits were quite big on us – especially on Em – but it didn't really matter. We slipped them over our cozzies. Mine was a funky lime green and black, and Em's was blue with a white zigzag pattern down the back.

"Go out in the water and stand where you think a wave is going to break," João instructed, giving me one of the boards. "When you feel it move under you, you jump forward. Let the wave do all the rest. Not too far out, remember. The current is strong here."

I wasn't sure what I was more nervous about: the body-boarding itself, or the fact that I would look like a total idiot in front of João if I fell off. I waded out to where Em was already paddling. I could feel the water pulling my legs. A wave surged under me and lifted my toes off the sand, so I jumped forward and gripped the board, feeling the swell rise and take me towards the shore. It wasn't very fast – until the wave broke, and I whooshed up to the beach so fast it made my head spin.

"I did it!" I squealed, my heart still racing with the rush I'd got from the wave. "It was brilliant. I'm going again!"

I waded out past Em as she sped into shore with this look of total concentration on her face. Feeling a bit braver, I pushed out further, until I couldn't feel the ground under my feet. I swam out with my hands on the board and bobbed there lazily, watching João on the shore as he waved at me and called something I couldn't hear. I could hardly believe he was waving at me. I waved back happily.

The sun was warm on my back, and holding the board was surprisingly comfortable. I just knew Mel and Lucy would totally *love* body-boarding. I realised guiltily that this was the first time I'd thought of my mates since we'd got here and I first clapped eyes on

João. That's love for you, I guess. I paddled my legs a bit, promising myself that I would write my mates a couple of postcards that afternoon.

The shore was looking rather a long way away. I was sure I'd only been a few yards off a minute ago. I glanced uneasily at the rocks that marked the end of the Castelo do Sol beach. I'd been level with them, hadn't I? How come they seemed ahead of me now?

With a horrible lurch, I realised that the current was pulling me out to sea. João had mentioned something about currents... I wriggled on to the board and started kicking for the beach. But it felt like I wasn't moving at all. In fact, it felt like the sea had other ideas and was pushing me further and further out.

Seriously panicking now, I lost my grip on the board. I sank under the waves for what felt like ages, but was probably just a few seconds. When I resurfaced, I couldn't see any land at all. Where was

the beach? Where were the cliffs? How come everything had disappeared?

I screamed. All I got for my trouble was a mouthful of seawater. *There's no sharks in the Mediterranean*, I told myself as I felt hysteria welling up inside me. But – this wasn't the Med, was it? It was the Atlantic. And the Atlantic went for thousands of miles and didn't end until America. Would I have to float around until I hit *America*?

I saw a flash of golden sand up ahead. Forcing myself to stay calm, I started paddling towards it. At last, the sea was being more helpful. The current was pulling me sideways, towards the beach. And then a wave rose up beneath me like a big humpbacked whale and I flew up the shore and crashed in a heap on to the sand.

I was so relieved to feel the sand under my fingers that I burst into tears. I didn't care if João saw me looking a mess. I decided right there and then that body-boarding was *not* for me.

"Are you OK?"

I stood up shakily. I could feel sand sticking all over my face. Standing there and looking concerned was a pretty girl in her twenties, wearing the most amazing bikini I'd ever seen. It was gold, all strings and straps, and looked seriously expensive.

"I... I'm fine," I sniffled. "I just..." I glanced around for João and Em. They weren't there. In fact, no one was there at all. Just me and the girl.

"You look like you've had a shock," the girl was saying. She sounded foreign – not Portuguese, something else. Her long blonde hair was done in corn rows all over her head, and she was wearing the most fantastic necklace that looked like it was made of coral.

I couldn't understand it. Where was everyone? The hotels had all disappeared as well. All I could see were these huge golden cliffs, the beach and this angelic-looking girl. How was this possible? Was this... Was I...

"Am I dead?" I gulped, my eyes feeling wobbly with tears.

The girl laughed. Her corn rows bounced on her golden shoulders. "Not dead," she said. "Just lost, maybe."

"Where's the town?" I stared around. "Castelo do Sol? It was *here*!"

"Next beach along," said the girl. She put her arm around my shoulders. "Looks like the current brought you around the corner. Come up to our villa. We'll sort you out and call your parents, yes?"

My parents. Em! Fresh tears flooded down my face. Feeling completely lost and awful, I held my board tightly against my body and followed the girl towards the cliff. A path suddenly appeared, cut into the golden stone. It wound up and away from the beach and the sea until we came out at the top.

The most amazing villa stood on the edge of the cliff in front of me. It was all glass and white marble, with flowers everywhere I looked. Two expensive-looking cars were parked outside the front door, which looked like it had been carved out of one enormous block of wood.

"Come in," said the girl, beckoning. "Your parents have a mobile number?"

I recited my mum's number. Then I put down the board and stepped through the door she was holding open for me. I stared in amazement at the curving glass staircase up ahead. Long cream leather couches stood around a massive fireplace. A kitchen with a black floor and sparkling glass tiles stood just beyond the living area, and out past the kitchen I could see a swimming pool.

The girl reappeared. She'd put on a long white silk robe that made her look more like an angel than ever. She held out her phone to me, smiling.

"Mum?" I said, my throat catching.

Mum burst into tears on the other end. It sounded like Em and João had run straight back to the hotel, and everyone had been going crazy with worry.

"It's OK," I said, trying to reassure her. It was weird hearing Mum so hysterical. "I'm fine. Just – can you come and get me though?"

The girl beckoned for the phone again. I handed it over. As she gave Mum a set of instructions on how to find the villa, I wandered into the kitchen. It had more gadgets than I'd ever seen in my life. I had no idea what half of them were even for. And the fridge was the size of a double garage!

The girl padded into the kitchen behind me. She opened the fridge and gestured for me to help myself to juice. "Your parents will be here very soon," she said. "And have a shower, if you like. It's at the top of the stairs. I'll find something for you to wear."

"Thanks," I stammered.

The huge fridge was stuck all over with Post-it notes, a calendar and several fridge magnets. One of them was the same as on our fridge at home. It was a weird little thing to fix on, but I found it really comforting.

The shower was like nothing I'd ever seen before. It didn't even have a tap – at least, not one I could see. Instead, it seemed to know that I was there, and jetted me all over with hot water. The sand swirled away down the drain. Stepping out, I saw a towel, and a little blue cotton dressing-gown had been put on the side of the shower for me. I dried myself and slipped into the gown.

The pale blue wink of the pool pulled me down the stairs again and through to the back of the villa.

It was huge, and the water at the edge looked like it was spilling away into thin air. You could see halfway down the coast from up here.

A noise from the pool made me look down into the water. A guy was doing laps, making hardly any splashes. His wet head appeared above the water every now and then. I did a double take. Was his hair *pink*? It looked like there was a stripe of pink running down the middle, from his forehead to the back of his neck. When he reached the far end of the pool, he turned and looked at me.

"Hi," I said, not sure what else to say.

He raised a hand at me before ducking back under the water again.

"Your parents are here," called the girl through the house.

I heard the crunch of car wheels on the stretch of gravel outside. Running back through the kitchen and past the big cream couches, I scooped the bag containing my cozzie and wetsuit from the girl's arms with a "Thanks a million!", jumped down the steps and hurtled into my parents' arms.

"I've aged a thousand years," Mum said, hugging me so tightly that I felt like my bones were about to snap. My dad rushed over and was now hugging the angel girl gratefully on the villa steps. "When Em told us you'd disappeared…"

"It's OK," I said, patting her on the back as she burst into tears again. Honestly, wasn't *I* the one who was supposed to be crying here? Em stared wide-eyed at me from the passenger seat as Dad took João's board from the girl with an extra-enthusiastic wave of thanks and climbed into the cab beside the driver.

"We thought you were dead," Em said, looking unusually serious.

"So did I," I said, and told them everything that

70

had happened as the taxi trundled down the drive, swung through a magnificent set of iron gates and out on to the main road back to Castelo do Sol.

"And the fridge had our tomato-shaped magnet on and the bloke in the pool had a pink stripe in his hair," I finished, just as the taxi turned into the road with the Hotel Paraíso on it. "It was like one of those dreams you get after you've eaten loads of cheese."

And then things got even weirder – Em started yelling at the top of her voice.

Six

"What?" I demanded, following Em as she raced up the hotel stairs to our room. "Em, what's going on? Why did you yell like that in the taxi?"

Em's whole body was shaking. She pulled open the drawer beside her bed and took out her football mag. Then she yanked open a page and stuck it under my nose.

"Yeah, the Marshalswick Park squad, I know," I said, feeling more confused than ever. "So what?"

Em jabbed the picture in the middle. It showed a nice-looking, dark-haired lad with a tilty nose and a diamond earring.

"You think that was *Carl Atkinson* I saw in the pool?" I said. Carl Atkinson was the Marshalswick Park captain. I recognised him from the posters Em had on her wall. He was actually pretty famous. Before playing for Marshalswick Park, he'd played at Benfica in Portugal, and even played for England sometimes. "But he doesn't have pink hair!"

"He does now," Em said. "He dyed it last week. It's in all the gossip mags. He's got a villa round here. It was definitely him! I can't believe you went in his villa, you lucky..." She stopped, looking horrified. "I can't believe *I* went to his villa and didn't even *see* him!" she wailed.

My legs started feeling all shaky again, like they had on the beach. I'd just been in a famous

footballer's holiday villa and hadn't even realised!

Em threw her magazine down on the bed and gripped me tightly by the arms. "Col!" she said. "You *have* to see Carl Atkinson again, and take me with you this time so he can sign my autograph book. We need a plan!"

Uh-oh. Em had that bulldozer look in her eye.

"How?" I protested. I had a bad feeling about this. "I'm not getting washed up on that beach again just so you can get an autograph, Em."

Em actually looked disappointed.

"Mum got the address so she could give it to the taxi man," I said, remembering suddenly. I looked down at the blue cotton robe I was still wearing. "And we have to take this robe back, I guess."

Em clapped her hands. "Perfect!" she said. "Let's go right now." She raced out of the room. When I didn't follow, she raced back again. "Well?" she demanded.

"There's just a teensy matter of putting on some clothes," I said sarcastically.

"Oh," Em said, frowning. "Right. Well, straight after that then, yeah? And *please* don't take a million years like normal, Col. I'll ask Dad if we can take another taxi straight back there!"

Not much chance of taking a million years with only about four things to choose from, I sighed to myself as Em disappeared again. Why hadn't the rep found my case yet? I sorted out what I had, and came up with a nice combination of white tee and miniskirt. I laced up my trainers, did my hair in a high ponytail and headed downstairs. Knowing Em, she'd already have a taxi waiting.

But instead of a taxi, Em was in the middle of a blazing row with Dad.

"We're *not* dashing straight back there just so you can get an autograph," Dad was insisting. He sounded feeble, even to me. You could tell that he was nearly as gutted not to have met Carl Atkinson as Em was. "They're on holiday, Em. They'll want their privacy."

"But we need to take the robe back!" Em pleaded.

"Of course we do," Mum said, reaching out to put her arm around me like she still didn't quite believe I was back. "But we can't just turn up unannounced."

"Call them and tell them we're coming," Em said at once.

Dad shook his head. "We don't have their number," he said. "Your mum's phone didn't register it."

Em glared at our folks. "You're not even *trying* to help me," she stormed. "It's only the most important thing in the *whole entire world*. Why can't we just drive up there and—"

"Enough," Mum said, in that sharp voice of hers that means exactly what it says. "We're *not* about to tear off back up the coast in an expensive taxi. We're

 76

going to have a nice dinner in the restaurant to celebrate Coleen's safe return, and we'll talk about how to get that robe back later."

"I'm not hungry," Em shouted, and raced back up the stairs to our room. We all heard the bedroom door slam.

"That went well," said Dad, scratching his head. He glanced at me. "Why did you have to wash up on a footballer's private beach, Coleen then, eh?" he sighed. "Couldn't you have picked a politician or a golf player or something boring like that? Now Em's got a right cob on – and knowing her, she won't drop it until we go and bother this poor lad for an autograph."

"Sorry, Dad," I mumbled. I was feeling pretty sheepish about everything now the shock and the excitement were wearing off.

"And on the subject of being sorry," Mum added, still clinging tightly to me as we made our way out to the restaurant, "you need to apologise to João. He said he warned you about the currents at the beach and told you not to go out too far. He's been beside himself ever since you disappeared, and he's got an earful from his parents about it as well."

I felt bad about that. I had a nasty feeling that there might not be any more trips down to the beach with João – not if he was in trouble with his folks.

As we entered the restaurant, I got swept off my feet by Mrs Santos, who wrapped her arms around me and planted two enormous kisses of relief on my cheeks.

"We are very pleased that you are well," Mr Santos said, looking extremely solemn.

I wriggled away from Mrs Santos and glanced across at João, who was standing by the bar and looking pale. "I'm sorry you were all worried," I said. "It wasn't João's fault. He did tell me about the currents. I just forgot."

João gave me a grateful smile as Mrs Santos made a move to hug me again.

"Dinner on the house!" Mr Santos announced. He looked like he was about to cry.

"Please, Mr Santos," said Mum gently, "you can't keep feeding us for free all the time. We know you've got a business to run."

Mr Santos bit his lip. "Very well," he said at last. "Free drinks then, yes?"

So free drinks it was.

Em joined us after about half an hour. She sat and kicked the chair and looked moody the whole time, even when we had ice cream for dessert. She only brightened up when we were helping João to clear our table.

"Do you know where the footballers hang out when

they're here on holiday, João?" she asked hopefully.

"Put a lid on it, Em," I muttered, though I knew I might as well be talking to a plank.

João shrugged. "They go to the expensive places," he said.

"Anywhere in Castelo do Sol?" Em pressed.

João stopped clearing the plates and thought for a minute. "There is Tony's, down near the sea," he said at last. "I know some of the people go there. I see photographers outside on the pavement sometimes."

Tony's. The name rang a bell. I frowned as I tried to place it. "The fridge!" I said, suddenly remembering. "There was a note on the fridge when I was at the villa. TONY'S – TUES 1PM, it said."

Em went white. "Tuesday!" she gasped. "Carl will be there! We *have* to go to that restaurant!"

I glanced to where Mum and Dad were chatting to Mr and Mrs Santos at the restaurant bar. Mum kept

looking back at me every couple of minutes, like she was checking I hadn't gone off to sink beneath the waves again. I could tell that she didn't want either of us out of her sight for a while. "They'll never let us go," I pointed out.

Em looked mutinous. "We'll sneak off if we have to," she said.

"What's with the *we* here?" I said, feeling cross all of a sudden. "What if I don't want to hang around a restaurant all day just in case we see your hero?"

Em looked at me like I was mad. "You've *met* him," she said, like me and Carl were best mates. "He *waved* at you."

"I said hi," I reminded her. "And he didn't say anything back. He just stuck his hand out of the water at me. You can't even call it a wave, really."

"Everyone knows you can't meet people unless you're with people they've met before," Em said, like this was the most obvious thing in the world. "So if I'm with you, you can introduce me because you've met him. And his girlfriend. She's called Marina, by the way. She's from Norway."

"Sounds like you'll be the one doing the introductions," I grumbled.

I knew when I was beaten. Em spotted it in my voice, and smiled triumphantly. It looked like we'd be at Tony's on Tuesday at one o'clock, whatever happened. So why did I get the feeling that this was a really, *really* bad idea?

Seven

The first thing Em put in her beach bag on Monday morning was her autograph book.

"We might bump into Carl today," she said happily.

I looked up from where I was fixing my miniskirt under my arms as a little top. It had an elasticated waist, so worked brilliantly. Reinventing my wardrobe every day from just six or seven different things was a whole lot more fun than I'd ever imagined it would be – though I did wish I had a different pair of shoes. "I thought we were doing the restaurant thing on Tuesday?" I said, making a note to myself to get Dad to badger the rep about my suitcase again.

"He might get hungry today as well," Em said. "Let's go and take a look at Tony's just in case. If Carl isn't there, then at least we'll know where the place is for tomorrow, and maybe find the best places to stand."

I wasn't going to get a second's peace if I didn't do what Em wanted. Deciding that half an hour spent with Em now would mean hours of relaxing on the beach later, I gave in.

"I'll come with you," Mum said at once when we asked her.

"Mum," I said, putting my hand on her arm as we all walked down the street together, "I won't disappear again, honest. You and Dad can relax. We'll be fine."

"OK," said Mum reluctantly. She glanced at the

golden beach which I knew was beckoning her. "We'll see you by the big rocks in an hour. Is your phone on?"

At last, me and Em were on our own. The beachfront was starting to fill up, and we could hear splashes and yells from the hotel pools.

"Let's go," said Em, and started running.

Sighing, I clamped my arms around my miniskirt top – it *so* wasn't designed for moving at speed – and followed.

The shops we passed were dreamy. Most of them had been closed the previous day, and it was great to see the doors open and clothes on the rails outside. I kept slowing down and peering at their cool marble interiors, where glamorous shop girls bustled around with armfuls of silks and cottons. I saw loads of brilliant sunglasses that I totally wanted, and some excellent beach shoes that would make a change from my trainers. But Em insisted that we kept on going.

"We might miss him," she said, marching on like those power-walkers we sometimes see in the park back home.

"He's not going to be having dinner at ten o'clock in the morning," I grumbled as I tore myself away from a whole window display of rainbow-coloured bikinis.

Tony's was almost at the end of the esplanade. It had smoked glass windows and a very discreet gold sign stencilled over the door. There was even a security guy at the entrance, wearing a dark red jacket and a pair of sunglasses. Two or three men stood around chatting on the pavement. They had cameras slung around their necks.

"Paparazzi," Em breathed, staring at the men in excitement.

"OK," I said. "We're here. Carl isn't. Happy now?"

"I want to go in," Em said.

I couldn't believe what I was hearing. "Carl isn't there," I repeated. "Why do you want to go inside?"

"I want to see if there's a good place for us to stand tomorrow dinnertime."

"What's wrong with outside?" I said helplessly. "That's where most people stand."

"I'm not most people," Em said. "And I want to see inside."

I eyed the security guard at the door. He was enormous. "I'd like to see you try," I said.

Em burst into tears. Horrified, I was about to put my arms around her when she rushed up to the security guy. "Please," she sobbed, "I really need a wee and I'm totally desperate and we don't know where our mum is. Can I use your toilet?"

The man took off his sunglasses and stared at Em, who was now hopping around like her feet were on fire.

"I'm busting!" Em wailed, her face all crumpled like a tissue.

He glanced at me next. Still recovering from the shock of Em's pure nerve, I smiled weakly.

"Sure," he said, and held open the door.

"Told you I could," Em said smugly as we stepped inside.

Everything was just how I imagined an expensive restaurant would be. The floor was marble, and the tables were covered with snowy white cloths. Huge abstract paintings hung on the walls, and these massive ferns stood in pots, screening off the tables for people who wanted a bit of privacy.

A restaurant manager with oiled-back hair was standing at the reception desk, talking to two waiters. Well, shouting is probably a better word for it. The waiters were staring at the floor as the manager yelled at them, jabbing his finger at their shoulders and then hissing for extra effect. He looked up and saw us staring at him.

"You kids," he said with a glare. "How did you come in here?"

"I need to use the toilet," said Em, and smiled at him. With her missing tooth, her smile was extra sweet just then.

"Out," ordered the manager, advancing on us. "Go out of here, now!" He flung open the door. Then he snapped something at the security guard before turning back to us. "We are not a public toilet," he said. "Go away, and do not come back."

"Really," I fumed as we walked away down to the beach. "What a horrible person. When you need a wee, you need a wee."

"Col," Em reminded me, "I don't."

"I know," I said. "It's just – I'm sure that's against human rights or something."

"Don't worry about it," Em said. "I saw the perfect place for us tomorrow. There's this bench behind one of those big ferns. If we sit there, no one will see us."

"Fine," I said, throwing my hands in the air. "So tomorrow, we just have to slip past the security guard again – who isn't going to fall for another wee story, by the way – and the snotty manager, and sit down in this hiding place of yours, and then we'll see Carl and have a chat and invite him to your next birthday party. Piece of cake."

"Carl's playing away at Liverpool on my next birthday," Em said, totally missing the sarcasm in my voice.

Sometimes I wonder if my little sister isn't my little sister at all, but some kind of alien who just happens to resemble a seven-year-old kid with a gap in her teeth.

Mum and Dad were quite groggy on Tuesday morning over breakfast. I noticed they were calling Mr and Mrs Santos "Antonio" and "Ana" now, and guessed they'd had a late evening together at the hotel bar after me and Em had gone to bed.

"Any plans this morning, girls?" said Dad over his extremely large cup of coffee. "Footballers to plague, tans to top up, waves to drown in?"

"Just beachy stuff," I said as Mum tutted at Dad. It was way too complicated to explain Em's plan just then.

"Great," said Dad. "I told Antonio and Ana last night that you girls could help João distribute some of these." He waved a handful of bright pink leaflets at us. "The hotel is going to have a beauty contest down on the beach football pitch on Saturday, to advertise themselves. They're going to provide refreshments so everyone can sample Ana's cooking – that way they should be able to drive trade back to

the restaurant. We need to get these out there and drum up a few competitors."

"Beauty contest?" said Em in disgust. "That's *seriously* naff."

I had to agree with Em. As a way of advertising the Hotel Paraíso, it was pretty weak. Who did beauty contests these days?

"It was Antonio's idea," said Mum diplomatically. "The pitch is booked and these flyers cost money, so I think it would be nice to show a bit of support. All you have to do is hand them out to passers-by. João will be with you, remember."

João was looking great today. He had his hair back in a thick ponytail that was even shinier than mine. Me and Em took a bunch of leaflets from the reception desk and promised Mr Santos that we'd distribute them all.

"Hotel lobbies are good places," João suggested

as we walked down to the front. "Also we can leave them on café tables, and give them to sunbathers on the beach."

"Yeah, yeah," Em grumbled. I knew she was checking her watch already, even though it was just ten o'clock and we still had three hours before Carl was due at Tony's for dinner. She'd taken to wearing her autograph book on a string around her neck, for extra-easy access.

We wandered up and down the front, chatting to the people on the beach and the waiters in the cafés (João seemed to know them all) and leaving the pink leaflets everywhere we went. At around eleven, João took us to his favourite café, where we had milkshakes and these really sweet, eggy cakes that you could buy everywhere in the town. Then we all had a bit of a kick-about on the beach with João's mates before we had to get back to our advertising mission.

The clock crept around to quarter past twelve. Em was starting to look really edgy. It said a lot for how much she liked João that she hadn't thrown down the last of her leaflets twenty minutes ago and marched off to take up position at Tony's for Operation Atkinson.

"Finished," João said at last as he handed over the last leaflet to a girl in one of the beachfront shops. "Thanks for your help." He looked at me. "You want to do something at the beach later, Coleen?" he asked.

Some of his hair had fallen out of his ponytail and was hanging over his shoulders. My tummy felt like melty ice cream as I looked into his dark brown eyes. He was just so sweet. Would anything ever happen with him? My first proper kiss?

"Later's fine, João," said Em, breaking the spell as she gripped my arm. "Right now, we've got to go somewhere."

I shrugged apologetically as Em dragged me away. "See you!" I called, and João waved.

"He is so gorgeous," I said to Em, feeling like a balloon on a string as my little sister tugged me along down the street.

"He still needs to work on his goal kicks," Em said as we reached Tony's.

Like it mattered!

Eight

"It's twelve thirty," said Em. She was so excited, her teeth were actually chattering.

We were lurking outside the restaurant, trying not to look too obvious. People were arriving for dinner all the time now – well-dressed people with expensive gold jewellery on their wrists and round their necks. It was at times like this that I really wished for my suitcase – and in particular for my sequinned sandals. I think I looked OK in my yellow vest, pink crops and wide belt around my waist. But

my trainers were looking more grey than white now.

"Have you got a plan yet?" I asked, pulling myself back from my gloomy shoe contemplation as the doorman stepped aside for two elegant businessmen who had just got out of a silver Mercedes. After two milkshakes, it was my turn to need a wee – for real this time. I hoped I could sneak into the toilets once we got through the doors.

"Yup," said Em. "We're getting new parents."

Taking my hand, she dragged me out from the white flowery bush we were hiding behind. We fell into step behind this couple heading inside the restaurant. They didn't notice. I ducked my head as we passed the guard. We were just kids out with their folks for a nice meal. Clever old Em!

Keeping our heads down, we sidled past the manager as he greeted our "parents" with oily politeness. I followed my little sister, my heart pounding like crazy as she darted across the restaurant. I was sure we were going to be seen at any minute.

Em shoved me behind this huge fern to where the little wooden bench was tucked up against the wall.

"This is crazy," I muttered, sitting down on the bench. My jitters were fading now I could see that we were hidden from the restaurant manager's view – although I still needed a wee. I glanced around for the toilets. To my dismay, they were right across the restaurant. There was no way I could reach them without the restaurant manager noticing.

"Now we wait," Em said. She was smiling so hard her face was nearly cracking. Twenty minutes until she saw her hero. Not long at all.

Let me just say here that twenty minutes is no biggie. I often wait for buses for twenty minutes, and with my music on and all my thoughts rushing around in my head, the time always speeds by.

But when you need a wee, twenty minutes is a *very* long time indeed.

There was a flurry at the door. Em stiffened. Then she squeaked with excitement. Carl Atkinson (complete with the famous pink stripe in his hair), the pretty blonde girl and six others had walked in. I forgot about my wee for about thirty seconds as I goggled at the girls' beautiful clothes. Carl's girlfriend Marina was wearing a fabulous silk kaftan in blue, white and green swirls. Her blonde hair streamed over her shoulders and her feet were tucked into a pair of killer heels. The other girls looked completely gorgeous too. I couldn't get over how shiny their hair was.

"...an honour to have you with us as ever, *Senhor* Atkinson," the restaurant manager gushed as he trotted along beside them, rubbing his hands in this real suck-up way. "Our *sommelier* has put your favourite wine in the cooler already..."

Em started giggling. "Did he say *smelly?*" she snorted. The excitement of being this close to her hero was clearly pushing her over the edge.

"Shhh!" I hissed, terrified that the restaurant manager would hear us. "I think it's a posh word for a wine waiter."

"*Smelly,*" snorted Em again, stuffing her hands into her mouth to stifle her giggles.

I prayed that I wouldn't get the giggles too. My giggles are mental. They burst out of me like a herd of stampeding buffalo at all the worst moments, and no amount of stuffing my hands in my mouth could ever stop them. Then I realised that there was no chance of giggling just now. I was too frightened that we were going to be seen – not to mention too busting for the toilet.

Em almost fell off the bench as the manager guided Carl and his party to the table right next to

 100

our fern. If we stretched out our hands and pushed through the foliage, we could have touched Carl Atkinson's sleeve.

"That's Fernand Delbier," Em muttered in a daze, clocking the other lads as they all settled down and ordered drinks. "And Lorenzo del Mar. And Alex Benbridge. Coleen! It's practically *the whole Marshalswick Park squad*!"

My wee refused to go away. I was getting that horrible full feeling. It was torture, sitting there and staring at the toilet door ten metres across the room. It might as well have been on the moon. Em, however, seemed ecstatic just to gaze through the fern at Carl and listen to the football chat.

"Can't you ask Carl for his autograph now, so we can go?" I pleaded in a whisper as the players and their girlfriends got their food. I wasn't sure how much longer I was going to be able to sit there without having a really embarrassing accident.

"We can't interrupt them when they're eating," Em whispered, still staring entranced at her hero. "It's really bad manners."

"Weeing on the floor of a restaurant is pretty bad manners too," I muttered, close to tears. What was I going to do? I focused on a menu that was pinned on a nearby wall. Perhaps I could memorise the dishes or something.

I had the starters and the mains off pat and was just desperately starting on the desserts when Carl called for the bill. The manager hurried up with a huge red leather folder, which he put on the table with a little bow. Carl opened it up and signed the bill inside, then slammed the folder shut and pushed it across to the edge of the table so he could pour himself a glass of water. The gust of air made by slamming the folder actually puffed the bill out and on to the tablecloth.

Unnoticed by the players, it floated off the table and landed in the middle of our fern.

"Carl's autograph," Em whispered, reaching for the bit of paper in excitement.

"You can't take that," I whispered back, snatching it from her. "It's payment for their meal. It would be like taking money, Em!"

Em pulled a face at me. I looked at the bill just before I went to slide it back on to the edge of the players' table. The amount at the bottom nearly made me faint. Then I looked again. The food looked even more expensive than I remembered. *Thirty-four euros* for a steak? The menu I'd just memorised had it down as twenty-eight.

"This isn't right," I said, running my eye down the bill and trying desperately to focus on the numbers over and above my busting bladder. Everything had six extra euros added on to it. Maybe it was service?

Mum always got mad about places adding service. She thought service should be down to the customers, not the restaurant – and I agreed with her. There's no way I would ever tip that snooty restaurant manager. But no – service was at the bottom, a swipingly huge one hundred and twenty euros. The only explanation was...

"I don't believe it!" I gasped. "That manager's trying to fiddle Carl!"

The manager was trotting back towards the players' table. He was rubbing his hands again – and no wonder. He was about to get more than two hundred extra euros out of them!

"*No one* cheats the captain of Marshalswick Park," said Em, in this completely furious voice I'd never heard before.

Words failed me as my little sister leaped to her feet. The players shouted with surprise, and the manager

 104

took several skipping steps backwards in shock.

"Don't pay, Carl!" Em shouted, pointing at the manager. "He's a lying, cheating *sleazebag*!"

"I'm so very sorry," flustered the manager as the players frowned at each other. "This is a terrible intrusion – I will remove this child right now–"

"Get off me, you *cheat*," Em growled, shoving the manager away from her so that he staggered backwards. "Coleen? Show them the bill!"

I rose to my feet, blushing like crazy. The players started laughing.

"Any more behind there?" remarked the player Em had said was Fernand Delbier.

Standing up was the last straw where my wee was concerned. I thrust the bill at Carl. "It fell off the table," I stammered. "Check the prices."

"I'm Em," Em introduced herself proudly to Carl Atkinson. "You're the best player ever. And this is my sister Coleen. You've met before actually..."

But I missed the rest of Em's introduction. As Marina put her arm around Em's shoulders and Lorenzo del Mar called over the sweating manager and demanded an explanation for the over-expensive steaks, I fled across the room to the toilet doors.

Relief at last.

Nine

So, how's that for embarrassing? You get a chance to meet someone famous – and what's more, that someone completely owes you for saving them money and getting one over a snooty, cheating restaurant manager. And what do you do? You run for the toilet.

I was still brooding on what a complete disaster meeting Carl Atkinson had been when me and Em pushed through the doors of the Hotel Paraíso to meet our folks.

"I've got Carl's autograph!" Em shouted, waving her autograph book at Mum and Dad, who were standing at the reception desk talking to Mr Santos. I don't know why she was saying it again, because she'd already shouted it down the phone at them as soon as we'd left the restaurant. "And Fernand Delbier! And Lorenzo del Mar! And Alex Benbridge!" She paused to draw breath. "And I've got Carl's mobile number too!" she squealed. "He said we could call him if we ever need a favour because Coleen stopped him from being taken for a mug, and Tony's won't be getting any more footballers' business because the manager is a complete sleazebag, and Carl shook my hand and signed my arm and I'm never washing *ever* again."

"I can't believe you interrupted their dinner," Dad began.

But Em was too busy squealing and running

around the reception to listen. João came out of the back and grinned at the sight of my little sister going crazy, while Mr Santos breathlessly asked to see Em's arm signature. Carl was pretty famous in Portugal too, having played for Benfica, the Portuguese club Mr Santos supported.

"Coleen," Mum groaned since she couldn't get Em's attention, "what were you thinking, letting Em in there to spy on those poor people like that?"

"Mum," I said wearily, "I couldn't stop her. You know what she's like. Especially where football is concerned. And *double* especially where Carl Atkinson is concerned."

"And I don't suppose you returned the robe either," Mum tutted.

I'd actually forgotten all about the robe. I shook my head sheepishly.

Mum didn't say anything else. She knew exactly

what I'd been up against. I think she felt a bit sorry for me, actually.

When Em finally calmed down, we all realised that we were totally starving. It was nearly three o'clock and me and Em hadn't eaten anything since the eggy cakes in the café that morning. Mum and Dad hadn't either, having been snoozing on the beach all day. So Mrs Santos set a table in the courtyard and brought us all delicious grilled sardines with buttery potatoes and salad.

"Your cooking is wonderful, Ana," said Mum as we munched through the charcoaly sardines with their crunch of sea salt. Mrs Santos smiled at Mum's compliment, and poured us all glasses of iced water. "I really hope this idea of the beauty contest and refreshments will bring in some more customers for your restaurant."

I'd forgotten about the pink leaflets we'd been

handing out that morning, and felt a sense of doom about how successful this beauty contest was actually going to be. It hadn't exactly been the idea of the century. "Has anyone called yet?" I asked.

"Three," Mr Santos sighed, hearing our question as he and João came out into the courtyard.

I exchanged glances with the rest of my family. Three? It wasn't going to be much of a contest, was it? The trouble with giving out leaflets was that people looked at them and instantly forgot about them. If people hadn't already called, I had a nasty feeling they never would.

"Three's not many," said Dad, shaking his head. "You should perhaps think of doing something else before it's too late."

"A football match for example," Em said, twirling her fork through her lettuce leaves. "Sell tickets to play or something."

I had been going to suggest a fashion show. But Em's words lit a fuse in my head as I thought of the most perfect, wonderful way to make money for the hotel.

"Coleen?" Mum said, looking worried as I choked on my potatoes. "Are you OK?"

I swallowed and breathed deeply, letting the wonderful, fabulous idea swim around in my head for a second. Then...

"How about a football match with a special guest?" I said, looking around the table with a grin. "A *very* special guest. A guest who said that he owed us one. A guest who gave us his mobile number just today—"

"CARL!" Em shrieked. "Coleen, that's genius!"

"Carl Atkinson?" Mr Santos echoed in astonishment. "You think he will come and play in a match for the Hotel Paraíso?"

"People would come to see him, *claro que sim,*" João said in excitement. "You really think he will do it, Coleen?"

"He said to call him if we needed a favour," I said. "So how's that for a favour?"

Em rifled through her autograph book with shaking fingers, looking for Carl's phone number.

"Here's my phone, Coleen," said Dad, looking like someone had just whacked him around the head with a stick. "Make the call."

Trying not to think about the embarrassing wee business at Tony's, I dialled the number before I lost my nerve. A familiar voice answered.

"Yup?"

"Hi, Carl?" I squeaked. Em made flapping gestures with her arms as she danced around the table. "It's Coleen. We er – met at Tony's today?"

Carl laughed. "Coleen, yeah – I remember you

and your sister. Ready for that favour already?"

He sounded so friendly that I relaxed. Crossing my fingers tightly, I told him about our plan. Em had sat down at the table again, and everyone was staring at me in this tense way.

"So," I said, "I know it's a bit cheeky, being your holiday and that, but it would really help our friends out if you played."

"Sure," said Carl. "Sounds fun. What time?"

I gave a massive thumbs-up to the others as I gabbled a time at him. Ten o'clock – the time Mr Santos had booked the pitch for the beauty contest.

The whole place erupted when I hung up the phone.

"A match with Carlos Atkinson," said Mr Santos, looking completely dazed. "For my hotel. I don't believe it!"

"Now all we have to do is sell the tickets," said

Dad with a massive grin. "Something tells me that won't be a problem."

And then everyone jumped into this huge tangled hug and our whole table got kicked over by mistake.

With just three days to go before the match, we had a lot to do. But advertising the match turned out to be totally unnecessary. João and his family told everyone they knew, who told everyone *they* knew, which basically covered everyone who worked in Castelo do Sol – including friends and relations who worked in the big hotels. And once the big hotels knew about it, all their guests knew about it. Talk about word of mouth. The phone at the Hotel Paraíso desk never stopped ringing.

We sat with the Santos family every morning at breakfast before heading out to the beach, talking about the plans for Saturday. Even though we were supposed to be on holiday, we were all dead keen to help arrange the match.

"So what food are you going to prepare, Ana?" asked Mum.

"*Sardinhas!*" Mrs Santos said. "We will grill them on the barbecue. On the fish I do a special *tempero* – how you say? Salt and spice?"

"Seasoning?" I suggested. My mouth was already watering at the thought of a barbecue.

"*Seesning,*" Mrs Santos said, screwing up her face as she wrapped her mouth around the English word. "*Sim,* yes."

We should auction places on the teams before the match starts," Dad suggested. "You know – highest bidder gets to play with Carl, not just watch him. I'll referee. I've got the right experience."

I had to laugh. It would be Dad's dream to order

116

players like Carl Atkinson around on the pitch!

"Don't sell all the places," João begged. "I would like very much to do the game. And my friends too."

"And me!" Em squealed.

Dad raised his eyebrows at Mr Santos. Auctioning team places would make a lot of money for the hotel. But it looked like Mr Santos had different priorities on this one.

"Of course they must play!" Mr Santos cried. "And I will play as well!"

By the time they'd listed all the friends and relations who wanted to play in the match, there weren't any places left to auction. But as tickets for the match were still selling like crazy and the money was flooding in, it didn't seem to matter.

The weirdest thing about the whole business was the way people we'd never met came up to us in the town and on the beach every time we went out. They all seemed to know exactly who we were, and what we had done for the Santos family. We were offered free coffee and cakes in the cafés, and had little gifts pressed into our hands on the market stalls. People said "*Ola!*" and "*Tudo bem?*" at us, which meant "Hi!" and "How are you?" Dad even got kissed on both cheeks by the guy on the beefsteak-in-a-bun kiosk. We were famous all over Castelo do Sol.

"This must be how Carl feels every time he goes out," I giggled on Friday morning, as yet another bunch of lads in wetsuits waved at us as they walked up the beach past our usual spot in the shade of the rocks.

"Hello," said Dad, opening one eye as a blonde woman struggled across the sand towards us. "Another fan?"

She looked familiar. Then I remembered. She was our holiday rep.

 118

"Nice to see you," Mum said drily. We hadn't clapped eyes on our rep since she'd left us outside the hotel.

"Yes," gasped the rep, adjusting her sunglasses on her sweaty nose. "I'm sorry we haven't been in touch. But good news! We have your daughter's suitcase!"

I sat up. "Really?" I gasped. I had completely given up on ever seeing my stuff again.

"We'll bring it round to your hotel today," said the rep. "I must apologise on behalf of SunFirst," she added. "I know you have been unhappy with the standard of your hotel. The next time you holiday with us, we'll have you in a sea-view suite at the Hotel Grande on the front."

"You'll do no such thing," Dad said. "We'll be booking direct with the Hotel Paraíso from now on. And I advise you to book more guests there in future. It's a little blinder of a hotel, and rooms are going to be like gold dust before long."

"But I understand there were problems with the towels..." the rep began.

"Nonsense," said Mum. "The best towels I've ever had. The best service and the best food. So report that back to your bosses."

The rep was now looking astonished. "I'm – we at SunFirst are delighted to hear that everything has been satisfactory," she said, looking a bit at a loss. "I'll get the suitcase over to you as soon as I can, and we'll see you for the airport bus tomorrow afternoon."

"I can't believe we're going home tomorrow afternoon," Em moaned as the rep struggled off across the sand again. "I wish you'd booked a fortnight, Dad."

"Don't worry, love," said Dad, resting back on his towel again. "We'll be back. You can count on that."

Ten

That evening I felt completely on top of the world. It was *fantastic* to see all my clothes again – and just in time for our last evening in Castelo do Sol.

"Are you ready yet, Coleen?" Mum called. "Antonio, Ana and João are waiting!"

Everyone in Castelo do Sol walked about in their best clothes at about six o'clock every evening. Tonight, we were going to join them. I carefully put on my gorgeous sequinned sandals and my best beach dress in the world (a long vest dress with an anchor on the front, in case you're wondering), and did my hair so it was loose and shiny on my shoulders, just like the footballers' girlfriends at Tony's on Tuesday. My legs had turned a lovely toffee colour, and I'd painted my toes in my favourite dark blue polish. It was brilliant to be able to put my trainers away!

João was looking really handsome in a pressed white shirt, and even Em had made an effort with a clean T-shirt and a pair of long red shorts that were only a bit crumpled. We all strolled down to the esplanade and along the front, listening to the twittering of the sparrows in the trees and the wash of the sea on the shore and checking out all the other people that we passed.

As Mr and Mrs Santos stopped with Mum, Dad and Em to chat with some friends at one of the bars, João

leaned towards me. "Coleen," he whispered. "Come down to the sea with me?"

My heart gave a massive lurch. I looked down at where João's brown hand had taken hold of mine. We walked together across the sand, which was golden in the evening sunlight. The beach pitch was all freshly marked out with chalk, ready for tomorrow's match, and huge banners hung all around the pitch proclaiming: "HOTEL PARAÍSO! THE FOOD AND ROOMS OF PARADISE!"

"You did a brilliant thing for my family this week," said João as we reached the water. "I think you are a fantastic person."

The sea was whooshing over the tips of my sequinned sandals. But I only noticed that after João had kissed me.

We were up at dawn on Saturday. We left our bags packed and ready in reception for our bus to the airport later (I'd only just *un*packed!) and went with the whole Santos family down to the beach, where a massive fishing net was being trawled into the shore by two tractors. It was really weird seeing tractors on a beach – but it felt like we were seeing the beach properly for the first time, as a place where the people of the town worked and lived and caught fish for their dinners.

We all watched, me with my arm around Mum, and Dad cuddling Em, as the fishermen wound the net right in and dumped a pile of glittering, slapping fish on the sand. Almost at once, the fish were sorted, gutted and divided up. Seagulls swooped overhead in a cloud of hungry feathers, cleaning up the beach like lightning. Men and women set up little stalls with portable scales for weighing the fish and selling them to customers who were already queuing patiently up the beach. The whole place was like an outdoor supermarket. It was *really* weird to picture it as it would look later, covered with sunbathing bodies and brightly coloured towels.

"The freshest sardines you will ever taste," said Mr Santos as we all moved forward to help carry the boxes of fish that Mrs Santos had bought for the food stall at today's match.

"Beats a tin any day," Dad joked.

By the time we got all the fish up to the pitch, it was eight o'clock. João was already lighting up a big beach barbecue beside a long table with knives and forks and paper plates, and several Santos cousins stood around the pitch, collecting tickets as people began arriving to get the best seats.

"Amazing," Mum murmured as we took our seats and watched. The place was filling up like a bathtub with the tap on full. By nine o'clock, the crowds were ten deep behind the actual seats.

"At this rate, the Hotel Paraíso will make enough money to build a pool for next year!" I said, which made Mum beam.

A group of kids had climbed a nearby rock formation, and were hanging off like monkeys with a bird's-eye view of the pitch. Three girls in bikinis turned up for the beauty contest and looked a bit confused when they were handed barbecue tongs and banners to wear that said "Hotel Paraíso – top of the league!"

At a quarter to ten, there was a roar of excitement. We all jumped to our feet, with Em rushing forward to see Carl Atkinson walk on to the pitch and gaze around with interest.

"*Senhor* Atkinson!" Mr Santos rushed forward and shook Carl's hand. "We are so very pleased to see you here! We cannot thank you enough for what you are doing today."

"I brought a few mates," said Carl, winking across at me and Em. "Hope that's OK?"

As he spoke, the crowd parted. Fernand Delbier, Lorenzo del Mar and Alex Benbridge walked out to join Carl. The crowd went nuts – Fernand and Lorenzo had both played for Portuguese teams. A few shouts of "Marshalswick Park!" roared around the pitch, proving that there were plenty of English fans around as well.

A ball was produced and the four players started tapping it around. João, Em and all of João's mates joined in, to roars of approval from the crowd. It was the most brilliant atmosphere.

"TV cameras!" I said to Mum, pointing gleefully towards a cameraman and sound guy. I recognised the logo on the side of the camera. They were English!

"My hotel, the Hotel Paraíso, is holding this special match with our good friend Carl Atkinson,"

Mr Santos was saying proudly to the camera. "The Hotel Paraíso can fulfil all your holiday dreams…"

"Good old Antonio," said Dad, pulling out his ref's whistle and bouncing it in his hand. "Looks like he's learned the art of self-promotion at last."

A burst of flashing cameras went off as Dad blew his whistle and the teams assembled in the middle of the pitch. Em had her full Marshalswick Park strip on and was bouncing around like Tigger on the wing, while Mr Santos threw off his jacket and revealed a Benfica football strip to shouts and whistles of delight from the Portuguese members of the crowd. Carl and Lorenzo were on one team, and Alex and Fernand on the other. No need to tell you which team Em had chosen to play for, right?

The match got underway. It was amazing the way the professionals played the ball. It was like they had glue on the tips of their shoes. The ball seemed to do exactly what they wanted, every single time. Carl gave a little demonstration of bouncing and holding the football on the back of his neck somewhere in the middle of the match before powering a goal straight past Mr Santos, and – after a busy half-time for Mrs Santos, the bikini girls and the grilled sardines – Fernand threw himself into a complete over-the-head kick to send a ball whistling past João's goalie mate Zeca.

"Em's got the ball!" I squealed as it kicked off from the middle again.

Sure enough, my little sister was powering towards Alex Benbridge. The top of her head barely reached Alex's waist as she feinted left, then right – got past him and tapped in a goal. The crowd went mental.

"We'll never hear the end of this," Mum informed me as Carl seized Em under the shoulders and lifted her up somewhere over his head. "And *imagine* your dad down at the Hartley Juniors clubhouse!"

The match was over. Carl's team had won.

"It gives me great pleasure," Mr Santos panted, still out of breath from running around the pitch, "to present the winners with these tickets to dine for free at our Hotel Paraíso restaurant. The best food in the Algarve!"

"If the food is as good as the food I'm eating right now, we look forward to it!" called Carl's girlfriend Marina, holding a paper plate of Mrs Santos's sardines and waving her fork in the air. Talk about free publicity! I saw that she had the cotton robe slung over her arm. Mum must've returned it to her at half-time.

"We've had a brilliant time," Carl said, waving to the crowd. "And I'd just like to say a special congratulations to our right wing." He nodded at Em. "A smashing little champ."

I clapped until my hands hurt, before deciding

that I would let my little sister crow for exactly half an hour after the match and then sit quite hard on her head. It would shut her up for all of two seconds, I knew, but still... I had a feeling two seconds of quiet was about all we were going to get from Em between now and Christmas!

Suddenly João was standing beside me. I beamed at him. "Great match," I said.

"*Sim*," he said with a smile. "Yes. A great match, and a great week." He stopped smiling then and stared at me. "It is sad you have to go today," he said.

My heart squeezed painfully. Our coach back to the airport was leaving any minute. I tried not to think about flying home and leaving João. Would I ever see him again? It felt so weird that, just a week ago, I'd been mooning about Ben Hanratty, Lucy's brother. Now Ben seemed totally unreal as I stood here holding hands with João.

"I'll email you loads," I promised, feeling two fat tears brewing up behind my eyes.

"OK," said João, looking happier. "Send me pictures of your home, yes? I would like to see it."

"Come and visit," I said impulsively.

"Maybe one day," João said.

Out of the corner of my eye, I saw the rep sidling up to Dad.

"The bus is leaving for the airport in half an hour," she informed him. "SunFirst hopes that you've had an enjoyable holiday with us."

"The best," said Dad, grinning inanely. And to the rep's complete surprise, he wrapped his arms around her and gave her a smacking great kiss.

Fab Funky Flip-flops!

Why not give your plain old flip-flops the
wow factor using one of these fab ideas!

ASK AN ADULT BEFORE YOU GET DECORATING

HAVE FUN!

You will need:

- ★ Plastic flip-flops
- ★ Waterproof craft glue
- ★ Scissors

One of:

- ★ Ribbon/wool/coloured string
- ★ Buttons/rhinestones/sequins
- ★ Feathers from an old feather boa
- ★ Fabric pens

PLEASE TAKE CARE WITH BOTH
THE GLUE AND THE SCISSORS!

Really Ribbony

Glue the end of the ribbon to the back of the flip-flop strap and then wrap it around to the front section and down the other side, gluing it down when you reach the end. You could try interweaving two different colours of ribbon, or doing the same with coloured wool or string.

Bring on
the Bling!

Glue an assortment
of pretty buttons,
rhinestones and sequins to
the straps, attaching the biggest
and blingiest to the front section
where the two straps meet.

Fluffy Fun

Cut feathers from an old feather boa,
trim them to size and stick them to
the straps for funky fluffy flip-flops!

Sole
Sister

Try drawing your own design on the soles and edges of plain flip flops with fabric or waterproof pens. Get creative!

VOILÀ!

YOUR FAB FUNKY FLIP-FLOPS

★ Top Tip! ★

If you have fabric flip-flops, you can sew the decorations on instead of using glue.

OUT NOW!
Book One

Passion for Fashion

Having a clothes crisis? Is your wardrobe a
style-free zone? Then maybe I can help. I'm
Coleen and I love fashion, friends and having fun.

We're putting on a charity catwalk show in
drama this term. Cue lights... music... and the
star of the show... it's me, Coleen! X

HarperCollins *Children's Books*

OUT NOW!

Book Two

Dress to Impress

Having a confidence crisis? Don't dare
wear that cute little mini-dress? Then
maybe I can help. I'm Coleen and I love
fashion, friends and having fun.

My best mate Lucy has got a hot date
this weekend and I'm going to transform
her style from drab to fab!

HarperCollins *Children's Books*

COMING SOON!
Book Five

Get ready to party in the next
sensational story from Coleen...

HarperCollins *Children's Books*